Octopus Escapes Again!

Written and Illustrated by Laurie Ellen Angus

DAWN PUBLICATIONS

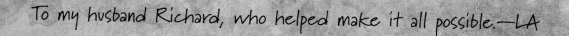

To my husband Richard, who helped make it all possible.—LA

Copyright © 2016 Laurie Ellen Angus

Illustrations copyright © 2016 Laurie Ellen Angus

Library of Congress Cataloging-in-Publication Data

Names: Angus, Laurie, author, illustrator.

Title: Octopus escapes again / written and illustrated by Laurie Angus.

Description: First edition. | Nevada City, CA : Dawn Publications, [2016] |

Summary: "Whether searching for its next meal or avoiding becoming a meal, an octopus is an underwater master through color camouflage, or by spewing a cloud of obscuring ink, or by sacrificing a limb, or squeezing its boneless body into or through unlikely spaces. Includes resources and activities for teachers and parents"-- Provided by publisher. | Includes bibliographical references.

Identifiers: LCCN 2016000275| ISBN 9781584695776 (hardback) ISBN 9781584695783 (pbk.)

Subjects: LCSH: Octopuses--Juvenile fiction. | CYAC: Octopuses--Fiction.

Classification: LCC PZ10.3.M2967 Oc 2016 | DDC [E]--dc23 LC record available at http://lccn.loc.gov/2016000275

Book design and computer production by Patty Arnold, *Menagerie Design & Publishing*

Manufactured by Regent Publishing Services, Hong Kong
Printed May, 2016, in ShenZhen, Guangdong, China

10 9 8 7 6 5 4 3 2 1
First Edition

Octopus is very hungry.
  She peeks to the right.
    Peeks to the left.
      And dashes from her den into the deep, dark sea.

Will she eat today?
Or be eaten?

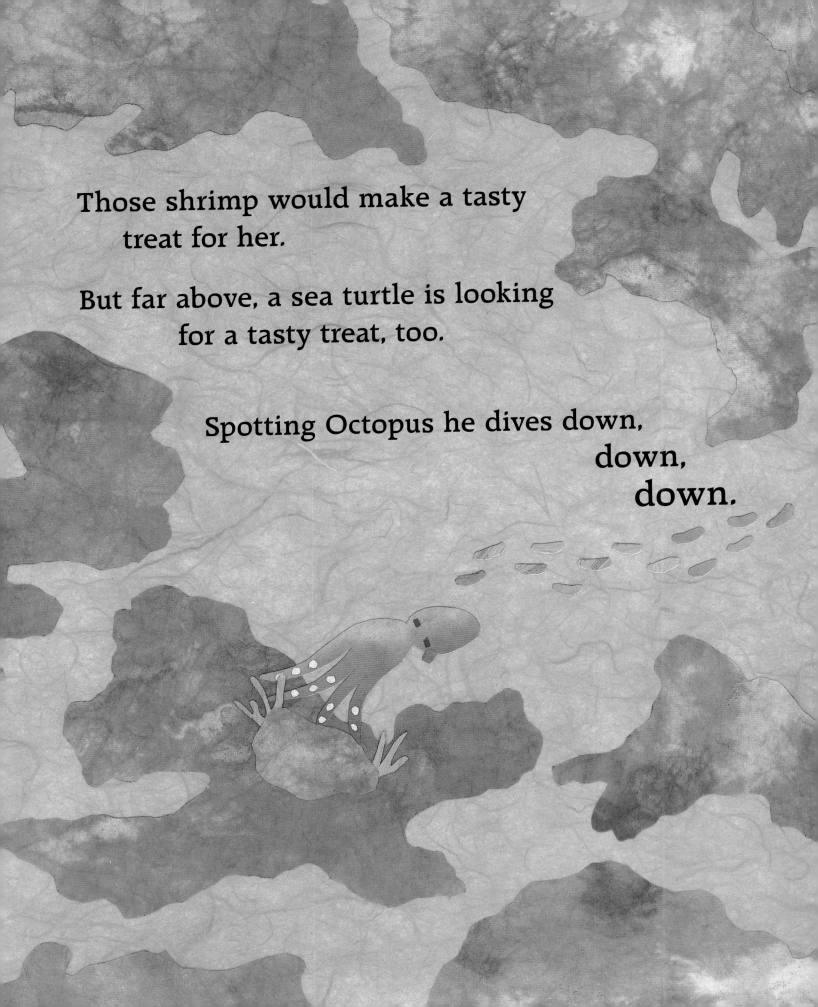

Those shrimp would make a tasty
treat for her.

But far above, a sea turtle is looking
for a tasty treat, too.

Spotting Octopus he dives down,
down,
down.

Quickly, Octopus
squeezes her soft body into
a nearby empty shell. A clever trick!

Octopuses have no bones, which makes them very
flexible. They sometimes squeeze their bodies into
empty bottles, cans, and even coconut shells.

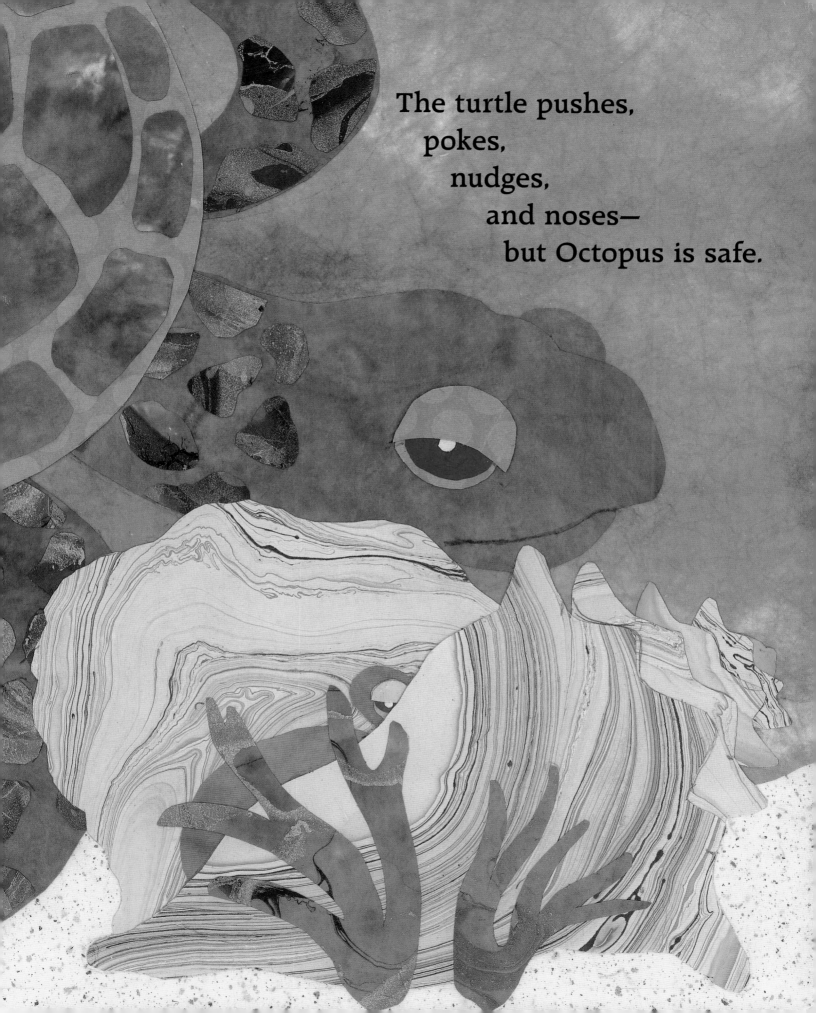

The turtle pushes,
pokes,
nudges,
and noses—
but Octopus is safe.

Octopus is still hungry. She swims alongside a school of fish.

One of her eight long arms reaches out to grab and gobble.

But wait!
Octopus spies an eel
slipping out of its cave,
ready to grab and gobble her!

Whoosh! Octopus releases her secret weapon—a cloud of dark ink.

She scoots away, still hungry.

When threatened, an octopus can spray ink.
This confuses the attacker and hides the
octopus, giving it time to escape.

Hunting for a shellfish or two, she glides
into nooks and slides into crannies.

But a prowling shark is hunting, too.
It spots Octopus and closes in.

Luckily for Octopus she knows
how to make a speedy getaway.

BLAST OFF!

When needing to make a fast escape, an octopus sucks in water and blasts it out through its siphon. The force of the water shoots the octopus away like a rocket.

Now Octopus is very hungry. She has a taste for snails.

But a giant grouper, lurking behind the sea grass, has a taste for Octopus. He opens his huge mouth wide to suck her in like a vacuum—hoping to swallow her in one giant gulp!

The grouper catches a
wriggling arm.
But only one!

Octopus escapes again!

When a predator catches an octopus by one of its arms, an octopus can release it from its body. While the predator is busy eating the arm, the octopus is able to escape. The arm will eventually grow back.

Still looking for a meal, Octopus crawls into shallow water along the shoreline. Slowly she sneaks in to grab a crab.

Uh-oh, a gull is swooping
down. Is it after
Octopus or a crab?
Octopus doesn't wait
to find out.

POOF!

Octopus disappears! She's a champion of camouflage.

Can you find her?

When threatened, an octopus can instantly change its color and texture to blend into its surroundings. And it becomes completely invisible to an attacker.

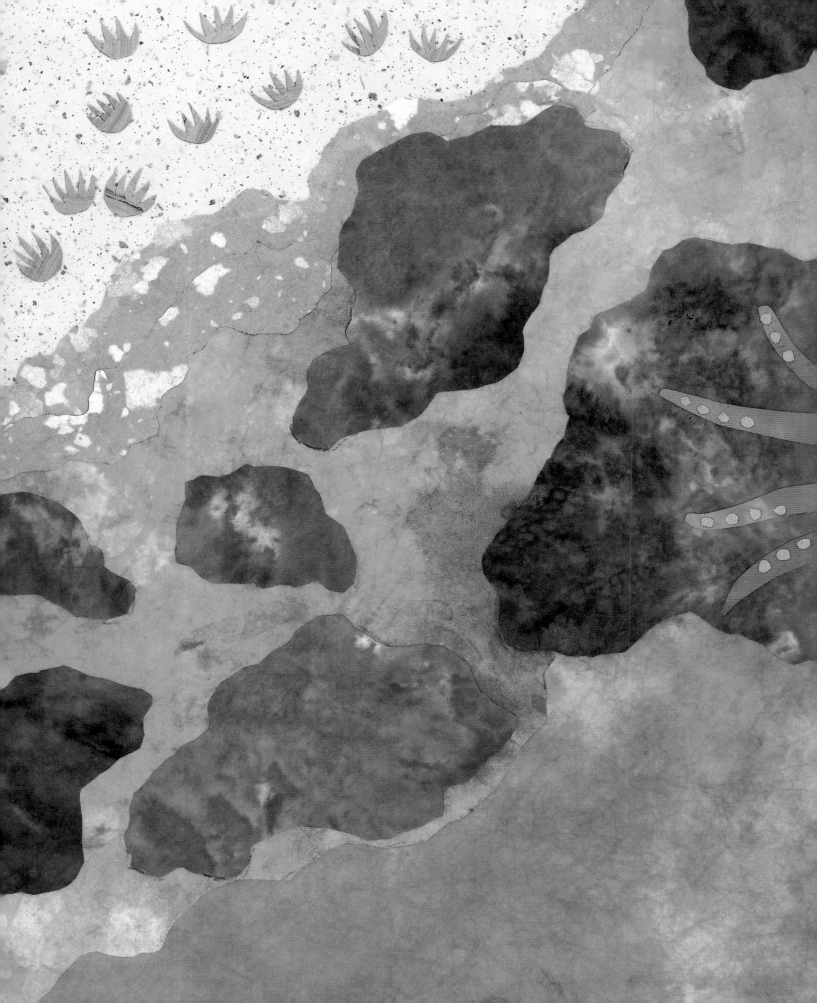

Clams would make a savory supper.
She dives back down into the
deep, dark sea, reaches out,
and scoops some up.

Finally—it's time to eat!

Welcome to the Wonderful World of the Octopus

There are about 300 species of octopuses. Some are so small they can fit into the palm of your hand. The record for largest octopus, a Giant Pacific Octopus, is 30 feet. That's almost as long as a school bus.

Octopuses are found in all oceans of the world. Some live close to shore. Others live far out in the ocean.

The word *octopus* comes from two Greek words meaning "eight" and "foot." Octopuses have eight flexible arms that are made mostly of muscle.

Octopuses don't have any bones. The only hard part of an octopus is its beak, which is part of its mouth.

Octopuses like to be alone. They spend most of their time hiding in their den—their home. They often create a den under a pile of rocks, inside a cave, or in a crack of coral. Some octopuses have used empty shells or glass bottles as a den. They usually hunt for food at night.

Mantle

Eyes

Siphon

Arms

Suckers

The octopus in this story is a Common Octopus.

It's about two feet long and weighs 6 to 22 pounds. It lives in shallow ocean water near rocky shores or around coral reefs. Like all octopuses, its body is perfectly suited for surviving in the ocean.

Is It Time to Eat?

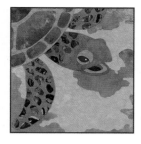 **Sea Turtles** live in the ocean, but they breathe air. There are seven different kinds. Some of them will eat an octopus. Adult sea turtles are mainly eaten by sharks and orca whales.

 **Eels** look like snakes, but they're not. They're fish. Moray eels slither through cracks and crevices hunting for food. They eat fish, squid, octopus, cuttlefish, and crab.

 **Sharks** have powerful jaws and rows of teeth. When a shark loses a tooth, another tooth soon replaces it. Sharks grow thousands of teeth in a lifetime. They eat animals like fish, octopus, seals, and even other sharks.

 **Groupers** are large fish. They're often over three feet long. They have chunky bodies and very big mouths. They eat other fish, octopus, crab, and lobster. They usually swallow them whole.

 **Gulls** live along the shoreline. They prey on mussels, crabs, sea urchins, and crayfish. But they'll eat just about anything, even human garbage.

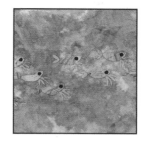 **Shrimp** live on the floor of the ocean. They have 10 legs and can only swim backwards. Shrimp eat tiny plants and animals that float on the ocean currents. Many ocean animals like to eat them, including humans.

 **Fish** swimming together in a group are called a *school*. Being part of a school protects fish from being eaten. It's harder for predators to pick out one fish from an entire school.

 **Sea Snails** travel slowly on one foot. They hide from predators inside their shell. They eat plants and animals. Sea snails are popular in aquariums because they clean up the algae that grows on the sides of the tank.

 **Crabs** have a hard shell that protects them from predators. They have ten legs. The first pair of legs is modified into large, grasping claws. They eat both plants and animals.

 **Clams** have two shells that are held together by a hinge. The shell protects their soft body. Clams strain their food out of sea water. They're prey for many animals, including humans.

Don't try to wrestle with an octopus!

Luckily for us, octopuses don't like to eat humans. They prefer fish, crabs, clams, shrimp, lobsters, and snails. And large species of octopus have even been known to eat a shark or two. With eight powerful arms lined with suckers, their grip is strong! It's almost impossible for their prey to escape once it's caught. **And that's not all!** Octopuses also use venom to stun their prey. Only the venom of the Blue-ringed Octopus is dangerous to humans.

My First Encounter

I've always been fascinated by the octopuses' amazing survival skills and how all its intelligence is stuffed inside a boneless mass of just eight arms attached to a huge bulbous head! So when my local aquarium acquired one, I was eager to see it up close. I've read much about the octopus, but nothing could compare to the experience of being just a few feet away from this brainy and alien-like animal. As I stood there, fascinated, she floated down from her tank and lingered, looking at me closely, seemingly as curious about me as I was about her. She then pressed one of her arms against the glass directly in front of me, to which I pressed my hand against the glass to meet her arm. Whether she was communicating with me I'll never really know, but I like to believe she was, and that this moment brought our very different worlds just a little bit closer. This lovely, inquisitive octopus inspired me to share her intelligence and clever abilities to survive in the dangerous depths of the ocean.

Structure and Function

Like all animals, octopuses have behaviors that help them survive. Their external and internal body parts allow them to see, feel, eat, grasp objects, protect themselves, and move from place to place.

Activity: Take a Closer Look

Octopuses are perfectly adapted for survival in the ocean. Refer to the labeled illustration on the "Explore More—For Kids" page as you share the following information with children.

 The **mantle** is a bag of skin and muscle that holds and protects all the organs, including three hearts and gills for breathing.

 A **siphon** (also called a funnel) is a tube-shaped opening in the mantle. When water is blasted out of the siphon, an octopus jets through the water in the opposite direction. It can go up to 25 miles per hour. That's faster than most humans can run! Ink also can be squirted out through the siphon from an ink sac in the mantle.

 The **head** is located below the mantle. It holds two large eyes, one on each side. An octopus has excellent vision, which allows it to find food and escape predators.

 Eight flexible **arms** are mostly muscle. They allow an octopus to grab prey. But octopuses are prey for eels, dolphins, sharks, and other large fish. If one of these attackers grabs an octopus's arm, the octopus can release the arm (called *autotomy*) and get away. The arm will grow back in a few weeks.

 There are two rows of round suction cups called **suckers** on each arm. A full-grown Common Octopus has about 240 suckers per arm. They can hold tightly to all kinds of surfaces. These sensitive suckers have nerves that send information to the octopus's brain. They help an octopus move, hunt, and even taste!

 A **mouth** with a beak is located where the arms join the head. This strong beak is similar in appearance to a parrot's beak. It can break the hard shells of prey. An octopus can also drill into shells to get at the animal inside.

Defense Mechanisms

Octopuses have a myriad of unusual ways to defend themselves.

Activity: Close Reading and Listening

Read aloud the story a second time and ask children to listen carefully to discover how Octopus stayed safe from danger. What parts of her body helped her?

 She squeezed into a small shell to avoid a turtle. She could do this because she is so flexible. Her body doesn't have any bones.

 Octopus used her siphon to squirt out a cloud of ink to confuse and escape from an eel.

 She jetted away from a shark by forcing water out through her siphon.

 When one of Octopus's arms was grabbed by a grouper, she released it and escaped.

 She camouflaged herself to blend into the environment to hide from a gull.

Intelligent Antics

Octopuses that have been confined in aquariums are known for their clever escape tactics. Here are some examples:

 An octopus at the Santa Monica Pier Aquarium disassembled the valve on her tank and flooded the aquarium with 200 gallons of water.

 An octopus in an aquarium in Germany squirted water onto a light above his tank, short-circuiting the lights in the entire building.

 An octopus in New Zealand escaped from its tank so many times that the staff had to tie the aquarium doors shut. Between escape attempts, the octopus hid in a drain for five days.

 An octopus in England learned how to squirt aquarium employees in the face with water.

 Octopuses in many aquariums have demonstrated their ability to unscrew a jar lid to get at the food inside. Watch a video of an octopus in action. Turn OFF the sound. https://www.youtube.com/watch?v=9kuAiuXezIU

Activity: Suction Cup Challenge

Have children work in pairs or small groups to try to unscrew a jar lid using small suction cups (available at craft stores).

Food Chains

Throughout the story, Octopus looked for food to eat (prey). And at the same time, other ocean animals (predators) wanted to eat her.

Activity: Who Eats Whom?

Review the story and identify which animals Octopus wanted to eat and which animals wanted to eat her. Create mobiles of an ocean food chain by connecting pictures of ocean animals with yarn, and hanging them in a line. You may introduce new vocabulary terms, such as *carnivore* (meat eater), *herbivore* (plant eater), and *omnivore* (both meat and plant eater). *Phytoplankton* (tiny marine plants) and *zooplankton* (tiny marine animals) form the basis of many ocean food chains.

Octopus-inspired Engineering Design

Solving a human problem based on a solution inspired by nature is called *biomimicry*. Scientists are taking inspiration from octopus skin to design hi-tech camouflage fabric. They want the fabric to respond to changes in lighting and coloration. These "octo-camo skins" have many military applications, including designing naval vessels that can sense the environment and blend into their surroundings. Other applications are for cars, toys, displays, and even living room walls that not only change color but also texture— going from smooth to bumpy.

Activity: Engineering Challenge

Have children choose one of the octopus's abilities and create an invention that will solve a human problem. Provide a variety of materials so children can create a model of their invention.

Suggested Videos

Seeing an octopus in action is an amazing sight. Fortunately, there are many excellent videos available online. This is a sampling of some of the best:

Scientific American blog: *Eight Great Octopus Videos*
http://blogs.scientificamerican.com/octopus-chronicles/eight-great-octopus-videos/

Science Friday *Where's the Octopus?*
http://www.sciencefriday.com/videos/wheres-the-octopus-2/

Discovery Channel *Octopus in Hot Pursuit of a Crab*
http://www.discovery.com/dscovrd/wildlife/viral-video-octopus-in-hot-pursuit-of-a-crab/

 **Don't Miss It!** There are many useful resources online for most of Dawn's books, including activities and standards-based lesson plans. Scan this code to go directly to activities for this book, or go to www.dawnpub.com and click on "Activities" for this and other books.

Laurie Ellen Angus grew up near the beach and could often be found knee deep in the water searching with delight for sea creatures to play with, such as horseshoe crabs, and also routinely chasing her younger brother around with them. Laurie doesn't chase her brother anymore, but does continue her fascination with the ocean, often taking long walks and observing the diversity of sea life along the shore. Laurie attended Parson's School of Design in NYC. Combining her love of nature and design into her artwork, she hopes to inspire children to have a similar fascination of the many amazing creatures that live in the ocean. Laurie lives on Long Island, New York, with her husband Richard, two quirky cats, and a rambunctious rabbit. This is Laurie's debut book.

Other Ocean-themed Books by Dawn Publications

On Kiki's Reef—A green sea turtle, Kiki, adopts the busy coral reef as her new home and discovers fish of all sizes and lots of surprises! But she returns to the beach—and the circle of life continues.

In One Tidepool: Crabs, Snails, and Salty Tails—One of the world's most fascinating habitats is at the edge of the ocean. Rhyming text takes children on a joyful and fantastical journey.

Over in the Ocean: In a Coral Reef—A coral reef is a marine nursery, teeming with mamas and babies. Children will count and clap to the rhythm of "Over in the Meadow" while reef animals flutter, puff, and dart.

Seashells by the Seashore—What works of art are shells! A lovely lilting rhyme takes children on a walk on the beach discovering beautiful shells along the way.

A Swim through the Sea—This is an illustrated tour of ocean plants and animals in an alphabet book format. It's a beautiful introduction to one of our planet's precious and fragile realms of biodiversity.

Pitter and Patter—A water drop is a wonderfully adventurous thing to be! Take a trip with two drops, Pitter and Patter, as they ride through the water cycle, meeting a variety of watershed animals as they go.

Granny's Clan—Life as a wild orca (killer) whale is a family affair. Here is the true story of Granny, a 100 year-old whale matriarch, who teaches young whales and helps her magnificent clan to survive.

John Denver's Ancient Rhymes: A Dolphin's Lullaby—In this illustrated adaptation of John Denver's song "Ancient Rhymes" you can feel the hope that birth brings—whether dolphin or human—and the promise of new life.

Salmon Stream—Follow the life cycle of salmon in cumulative verse. Against staggering odds, salmon hatch and grow, travel to the ocean, and eventually struggle upstream to spawn a new generation.

Earth Heroes: Champions of the Oceans—Eight short stories introduce upper elementary and middle school children to conservationists who explored the seas and worked to save ocean animals. Hopeful and inspiring!

Dawn Publications is dedicated to inspiring in children a deeper understanding and appreciation for all life on Earth. You can browse through our titles, download resources for teachers, and order at www.dawnpub.com or call 800-545-7475.